A TEMPLAR BOOK

First published in the UK in 2008 by Templar Publishing,
an imprint of The Templar company plc,
The Granary, North Street, Dorking, Surrey, RH4 1DN
www.templarco.co.uk

copyright © 2008 by Kevin Waldron

First edition

ISBN 978-1-84011-898-8

Edited by Ruth Martin

Printed in Hong Kong

MR PEEK
AND THE MISUNDERSTANDING
AT THE ZOO

BY KEVIN WALDRON

templar publishing

IT IS ON THE STROKE OF 9AM, MORE OR LESS,
THAT **MR PEEK** THE ZOOKEEPER
GETS READY TO DO HIS ROUNDS.
HE PUTS ON HIS FAVOURITE JACKET -
IT MAKES HIM FEEL VERY IMPORTANT.

HE NOTICES THAT IT IS **VERY** TIGHT
AND ONE OF THE BUTTONS **POPS OFF!**
THIS IS NOT A GOOD START TO HIS DAY
BUT HE SETS OFF NONETHELESS.

"It's only a
button!"

"Oh woe is me! You're getting very fat,"

MR PEEK SAYS TO **HIMSELF**, NOTICING THE BULGE IN HIS JACKET.

THE **HIPPO** OVERHEARS AND THINKS THE REMARK IS INTENDED FOR **HER!**

"All that terrible food you eat will be the end of you!"

MR PEEK PROCLAIMS AS HE PASSES THE PENGUIN'S POOL. HEARING WHAT HE SAID, THE PENGUINS ALL LOOK AT EACH OTHER **IN HORROR**. THEY HAD **JUST** FINISHED BREAKFAST!

"Why, you're sweating just doing your rounds,"

MR PEEK SAYS TO HIMSELF AS HE APPROACHES THE BEAR'S CAVE.

"You stink!"

HE EXCLAIMS.

"You're getting old too – look how wrinkly you are,"

DECLARES MR PEEK **TO HIMSELF**
AS HE PASSES THE ELEPHANTS.

"If they think you're too old for this job, they'll fire you!"

HE SIGHS AS HE PASSES THE **CROCODILE** PIT.

MR PEEK CHECKS ON THE **MONKEYS**,
MUTTERING TO HIMSELF,
"They're all out to get you."

"You can't turn your back for a moment!"

"Maybe it won't even come to that,"

HE **SULKS** TO HIMSELF AS HE NEARS
THE **TORTOISE'S** GARDEN,

"You could get run down by a rhino tomorrow!"

"Would anybody even care?"

MR PEEK ASKS HIMSELF ALOUD,
SURROUNDED BY GIRAFFES.

"None of the animals even like you!"

"Oh, woe is me!"

MR PEEK CONTINUES, FEELING VERY SORRY FOR HIMSELF.

TURNING A CORNER, HE SEES HIS SON **JIMMY**
SWEEPING THE PATH IN A **VERY LARGE** JACKET
THAT REACHES **DOWN** TO THE GROUND.

MR PEEK AND JIMMY SWAP THEIR JACKETS.
JIMMY'S JACKET IS **MISSING A BUTTON**,
BUT HE CAN SEE THE FUNNY SIDE OF IT.
MR PEEK IS VERY RELIEVED.

"See you at home for lunch, son."

HE SAYS **CHEERILY**,
AND SETS OFF AGAIN.

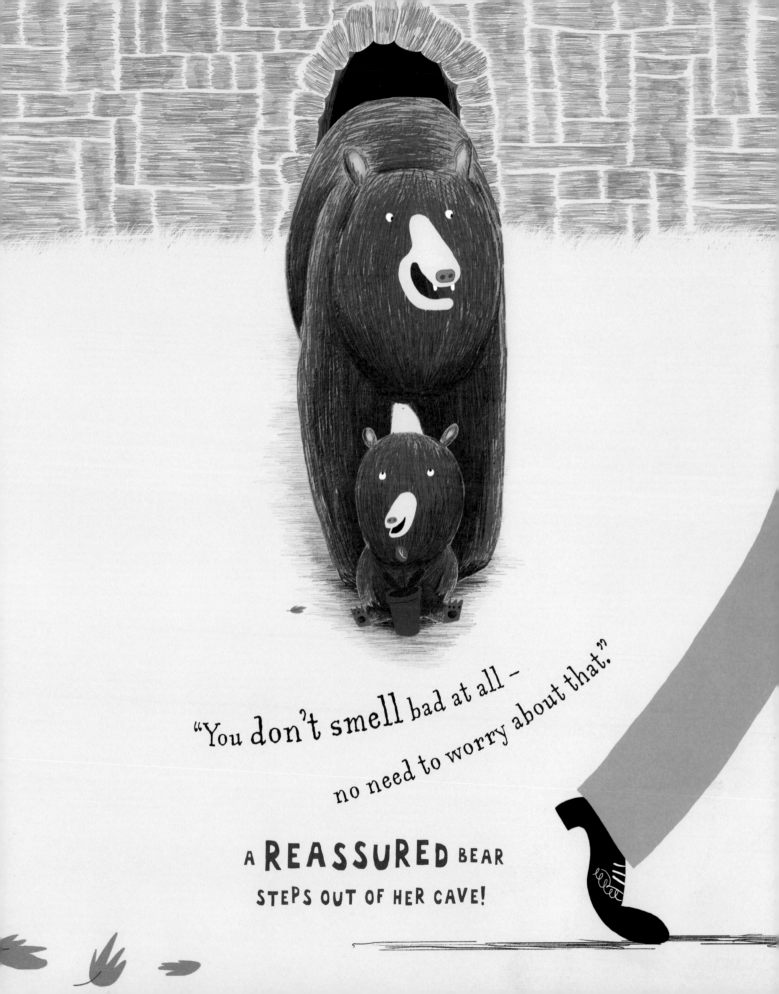

"You don't smell bad at all –
no need to worry about that."

A **REASSURED** BEAR
STEPS OUT OF HER CAVE!

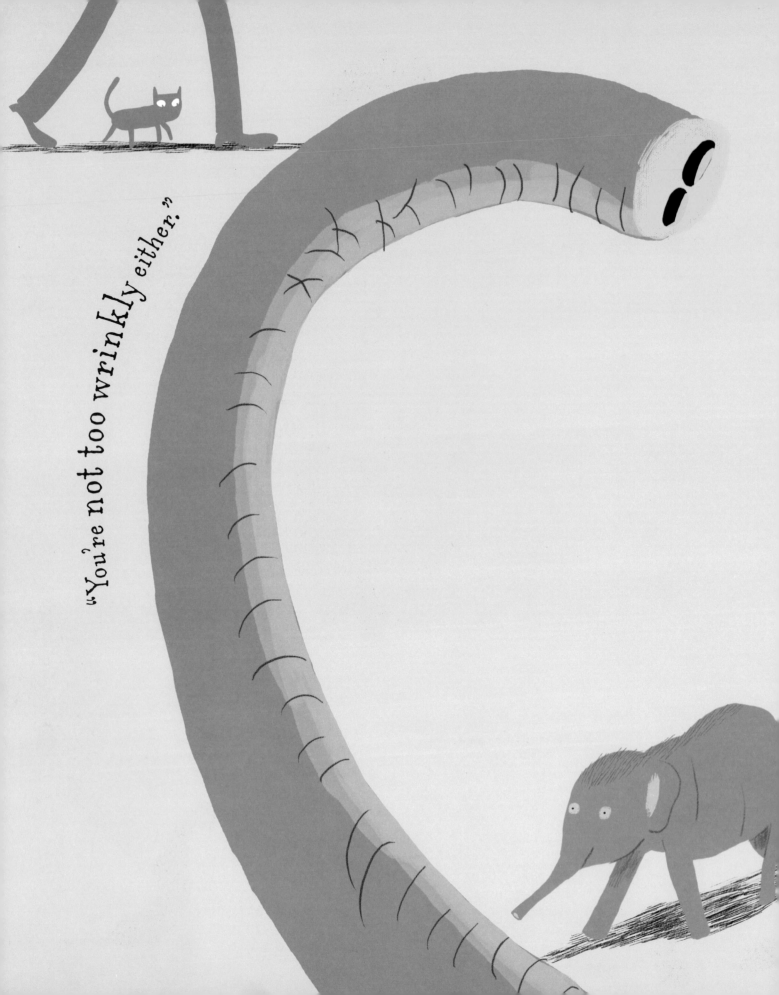

"You're not too wrinkly either."

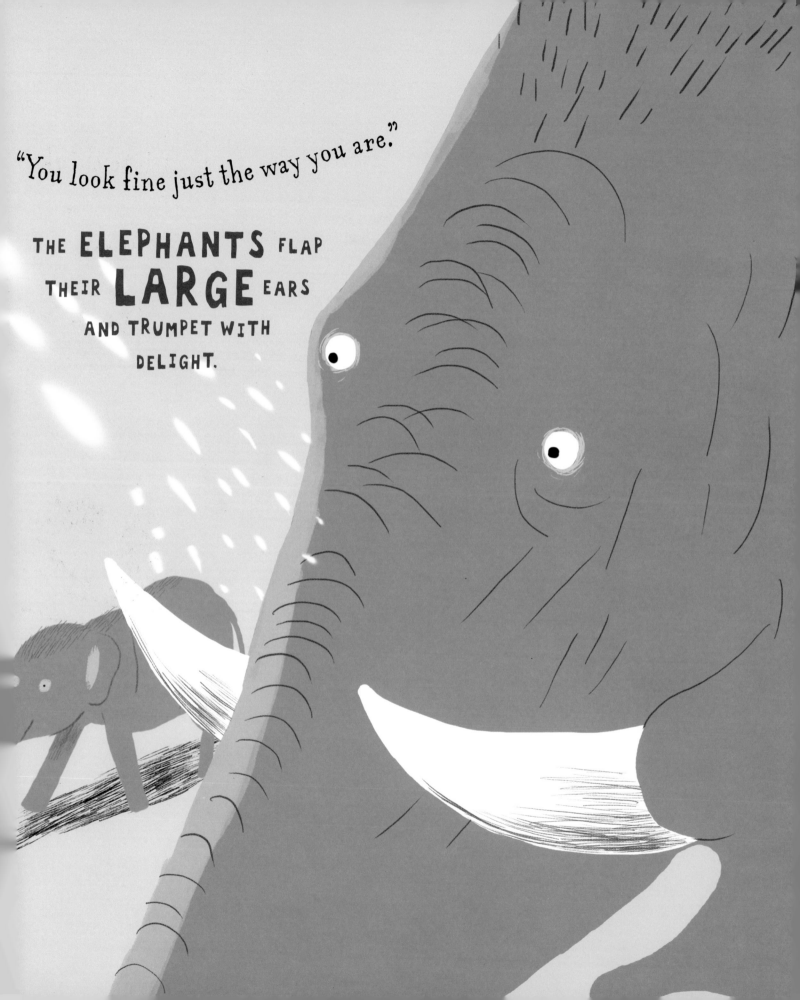

"You look fine just the way you are."

THE **ELEPHANTS** FLAP THEIR **LARGE** EARS AND TRUMPET WITH DELIGHT.

"You were foolish to think that they are always watching you!"

WHEN THE CROCODILES **HEAR** THIS THEY **RELAX** AND **LAUGH** AT THEMSELVES.

THE **GiRAFFES** WERE STILL FEELING **BLUE**,

UNTIL MR PEEK PASSED BY AND SAID...

"All the animals
are like family to you.
There is no reason
to **doubt** that."

"All's well with the world,"

THOUGHT MR PEEK, **PLEASED** TO SEE
THE ANIMALS LOOKING SO CHEERFUL.
HE HAD THOUGHT THEY LOOKED A
LITTLE **GLUM** EARLIER ON...

MR PEEK PROMISED HIMSELF THAT HE
WOULDN'T GET **SO CARRIED AWAY** AGAIN.
HE REACHED INTO HIS POCKET
FOR HIS KEYS...

BUT THEY WERE **NOT** THERE!

"Oh poop! those mischievous monkeys – they must have picked my pockets!"